Uncle Wiggily
and the Sugar Cookie

by Howard R. Garis

Illustrated by Aldren Watson

Platt & Munk, Publishers/New York

Once upon a time, Uncle Wiggily set out in search of an adventure. On his way out the door of the hollow stump bungalow, Nurse Jane Fuzzy Wuzzy, the dear muskrat lady, stopped him.

"While you are out looking for adventure, Uncle Wiggily, I'd like you to pick up something at the store. And for fear you may forget it, I have written the name of it on this sugar cookie."

"Ha! What a very good idea!" chuckled Uncle Wiggily, as he put it in his pocket. "I'll be sure to remember. Good-bye for awhile!"

And away he hopped, over the fields and through the woods. All of a sudden, he heard a rustling in the bushes.

"Why, Sammie Littletail!" cried Uncle Wiggily. "What are you doing here?"

"I'm looking for a mud puddle," answered Sammie.

"A mud puddle! Whatever for?" cried the rabbit gentleman.

"I just got these new rubber boots, and I want to test them for leaks."

Into the meadow hopped Uncle Wiggily and
Sammie, and, sure enough, there was just the nicest
mud puddle for which a heart could wish. It was all
squidgie-squodgie, mucky mud, with a pool of water
at the center.

As Uncle Wiggily watched Sammie wading out from shore, he reached into his pocket for the cookie. But just as he took a bite, he saw the pink candy letters.

"You're doing ever so well, Sammie," he said. "But
I just remembered I have to go to the store for
Nurse Jane. Wait here until I come back."
And away hopped Uncle Wiggily.

Just as Uncle Wiggily made his purchase at the store,
Mrs. Moo Cow came running in, crying:
"Hurry, Uncle Wiggily. Hurry and help Sammie!

He's stuck in the mud puddle with his new boots,
and he can't get out!" mooed Mrs. Cow.
Uncle Wiggily ran to the rescue.

"Sammie!" cried Uncle Wiggily. "Jump out of your boots and wade over here in your stocking feet."

"No! No, indeed!" cried Sammie. "Do you think I'm going to leave my new boots stuck in the mud? I won't come out unless they do."

Uncle Wiggily held out a fence rail across the mud
puddle. Sammie grasped it in his front paws. There
was a long strong pull. There was a squidgie-squodgie
sound, as the boots and the rabbit boy in them were
pulled out of the sticky mud.

Sammie giggled and blushed.
"At least my boots don't leak. Thank you, Uncle Wiggily! But, oh, Uncle Wiggily, look what's coming! Look! Look!" cried Sammie.

Out from behind a big rock came the bad Bob Cat
and caught Uncle Wiggily. "I want ears!" he howled.

"Excuse me," said Uncle Wiggily, "but your claws need cutting!" And taking from his pocket the long pair of scissors which he had bought for Nurse Jane, he began to trim the bad Bob Cat's nails.

The bad Bob Cat was so terrified (no one had ever before trimmed his nails) that he ran off into the woods and didn't come back for a long, long time.

And so Uncle Wiggily drove away the Bad Chap that tried to nibble his ears, and everything came out all right, for which I am very thankful, and I hope you are, too.

Then he helped Sammie wash the mud off his new boots and gave the rabbit boy a piece of the sugar cookie he had saved. And that's the end of the story. And if the bathtub doesn't go downstairs and stay out on the front porch to scare the milkman when he brings us the chocolate cake, I'll be back to tell you another adventure.